PUFFIN BOC

Bubblegum

Other books by Wendy Smith

THE FIT FAT CAT
THE WITCH BABY

With Margaret Mahy

KEEPING HOUSE
MAKING FRIENDS

Other titles in the First Young Puffin series

BELLA AT THE BALLET Brian Ball
BLESSU Dick King-Smith
THE DAY THE SMELLS WENT WRONG Catherine Sefton
DUMPLING Dick King-Smith
THE INCREDIBLE SHRINKING HIPPO Stephanie Baudet
SOS FOR RITA Hilda Offen
WHAT STELLA SAW Wendy Smith

Bubblegum
Bother

Written and illustrated by
Wendy Smith

PUFFIN BOOKS

PUFFIN BOOKS

Published by the Penguin Group
Penguin Books Ltd, 27 Wrights Lane, London W8 5TZ, England
Penguin Books USA Inc., 375 Hudson Street, New York, New York 10014, USA
Penguin Books Australia Ltd, Ringwood, Victoria, Australia
Penguin Books Canada Ltd, 10 Alcorn Avenue, Toronto, Ontario, Canada M4V 3B2
Penguin Books (NZ) Ltd, 182–190 Wairau Road, Auckland 10, New Zealand

Penguin Books Ltd, Registered Offices: Harmondsworth, Middlesex, England

First published by Hamish Hamilton Ltd 1994
Published in Puffin Books 1995
3 5 7 9 10 8 6 4 2

Film set in 15pt Plantin

PRINTED IN BELGIUM BY

INTERNATIONAL BOOK PRODUCTION

Bobby loved bubblegum. He loved sucking
and chewing it, turning the gum round and
round in his mouth till the flavour
completely disappeared. Then he blew it
into huge balloons, and carried on blowing
until they burst. Pop, splat, flump!

Even better, he loved hiding the tasteless blobs where his family would never expect to find them.

"That's disgusting, Bobby!" said his mum, scraping a ball of pink squidge from her shoe.

"How could you?" squealed his sister Judy, prising gum off the soap.

"Waagh!" screeched the cat as she tried to lick her tail clean.

"That's enough!" said his father sternly, when he couldn't unstick his newspaper. "No more bubblegum in this house. Now, go to school."

As soon as he turned the corner, Bobby popped some fresh gum into his mouth. There was no way he was going to give up blowing bubbles. Not for nothing was he known as Bubbles, the Champion Balloon Blower. No one could blow bubbles as big as he could, not even his best friend, Blue.

Blue was waiting for him at the school gate.

"Here, Bubbles," he cried, handing Bobby a strip of gum. "Try this. It's new. We'll have a bubble-blowing contest in Nature class, but we must make sure Miss Harley doesn't catch us."

Bobby looked at the gum.

It was a pity he didn't
bother to look at the small print, which read,
'WARNING – DO NOT CHEW WITH
FIZZY DRINKS. DO *NOT* SWALLOW.'

"Mmm," said Bobby, as the sharp tastes
exploded on his tongue.

"It's good," said Blue, trying to chew as
fast as Bobby.

They were so busy making bubbles they
did not notice Miss Harley approaching
with a jar of tadpoles.

"I've warned you about this disgusting
habit before," said Miss Harley. "Spit out
that bubblegum at once!"

Blue spat his out into the gum wrapper. Bobby just pretended to, it was far too good to throw away. When Miss Harley wasn't looking, he dropped Blue's gum into the tadpole jar and carried on chewing his own, wondering all the while just how magical a bubble he could blow.

The gum lasted all through Nature,
morning break and History. It was still
going strong when the dinner bell rang. The
flavour was growing more and more
delicious, instead of fading away as it
usually did.

Bobby wasn't going to let food spoil his fun. He swigged down some coke and continued to chew. All through lunch he worked the gum, till it was ready to blow into the biggest bubble ever made in history. He should just be able to manage it before the afternoon lessons started.

Blue watched Bobby's chipmunk cheeks in admiration.

"It's going to be a whopper," he said,
giving him a playful thump on the back.

"MEGA MAGIC," gulped Bobby,
swallowing the gum whole. To his alarm,
he let out a loud whistle as the gum sped
down his throat.

"I've read that bubblegum's harmless,"
he told Blue, as they walked to the gym,
hoping it was true. "I've swallowed it
millions of times, and nothing's ever
happened."

And at first, nothing did happen. The class swung on ropes, did exercises on mats, and then they skipped. Wip! Wap! went Bobby's ropes. He was the fastest in the class.

As he skipped, he began to feel peculiar. His ankles began to swell. His stomach began to bulge. He felt fat all over. He started to skip higher. Higher than he meant to. He skipped clean out of the window and up into the sky.

A light wind twirled him round so that he was floating on his stomach, and could see the whole school rushing out and gathering beneath him.

"Look at Bubbles," they screamed in delight.

Bobby managed to give them a wave with one pudgy hand.

The view was wonderful but it was cold so high up, and suddenly Bobby didn't like the taste of raspberry and pickles any more.

A fire-engine and ambulance had been summoned. Standing on the school roof, Mr Straw, the Headmaster, prepared to shoot his bow and arrow.

"It's the only way to save the silly boy," he muttered. "Hurry, children, and put that trampoline just here!"

"Wait!" cried Blue. "I have a magical rescue plan!"

Swiftly, he unwrapped and swallowed three strips of Magical Bubble Gum, drowning it with coke (*he* had read the small print on the wrapper). Tying the Mountaineering Club's rope to his left leg and securing one end to the school cook, Blue skipped into the air.

"Oh, do give him a hand, children," insisted Miss Harley. "Everybody, blow."

The whole school drew breath and blew Blue into the air, watching goggle-eyed as he floated up to Bobby.

"Hold on, Bubbles!" screamed Blue, dog-paddling in the air.

"Go on, Blue!" the school shouted up from below.

Flapping his arms madly, he just managed to reach Bobby when a sudden gust of wind blew him cruelly back to where he had started.

"Blow everybody, blow," Miss Harley ordered.

Everyone blew.

"Harder!" she commanded.

They blew harder and harder. All of a sudden, Blue whooshed like a rocket to Bobby's side.

There was just enough rope for Blue to tie Bobby to him. At once, Miss Harley began to haul them in, and gracefully, the two fat boys came sailing down, huge bubbles emerging from their mouths.

Mr Straw saw his chance. As the boys hovered over the roof, he deftly twanged his bow, shooting the arrows directly on target. Pop! Splat! Flump! Their bubbles burst, Bobby and Blue zig-zagged across the playground, plopping straight into the school waste-bins.

There they stayed, stuck fast, till the
Magical Bubble Company biked over a jar
of their Magical De-Bubbling paste.

"Well, that was fun, boys," said Mr Straw. "Quite a school first, I'd say."

"Just the ticket," said Miss Harley (who had by now discovered her bubble-blowing tadpoles), "for a fund-raising event at the school fête."

And that is how Bobby invented the new sport of Gum Gliding, which was to become hugely popular at the Summer Fayre, raising hundreds and hundreds of pounds for the School Archery Club.

Sadly, it was the first and last event of its kind, because, soon after, the Magical Bubble Company went bust (that means ran out of money).

"Too long-lasting flavour."

"Too much bubble."

"Too little profit," said the Directors, closing the gum factory down.

So Bubbles discovered a new hobby to use up his immense lung power. And his family never could decide which was worse.

P.S. The cat, who was stone deaf, loved it!

Also available in First Young Puffin

WHAT STELLA SAW
Wendy Smith

Stella's mum is a fortune-teller who always gets things wrong. But when football-mad Stella starts reading tea-leaves, she seems to be right every time!
Or is she . . .

THE DAY THE SMELLS WENT WRONG
Catherine Sefton

It is just an ordinary day, but Jackie and Phil can't understand why nothing smells as it should. Toast smells like tar, fruit smells like fish, and their school dinners smell of perfume! Together, Jackie and Phil discover the cause of the problem . . .

BELLA AT THE BALLET
Brian Ball

Bella has been looking forward to her first ballet lesson for ages – but she's cross when Mum says Baby Tommy is coming with them. Bella is sure Tommy will spoil everything, but in the end it's hard to know who enjoys the class more – Bella or Tommy!